Michael Arvaarluk Kusugak
HIDE AND SNEAK
Vladyana Krykorka

Annick Press Ltd.
Toronto • New York • Vancouver

©1992 Michael Arvaarluk Kusugak (text)
©1992 Vladyana Krykorka (illustrations)
Graphic design by Vladyana Krykorka

Sixth printing, September 2000

Annick Press Ltd.

We acknowledge the support of the Canada Council for the Arts,
the Ontario Arts Council, and the Government of Canada through
the Book Publishing Industry Development Program (BPIDP)
for our publishing activities.

Cataloguing in Publication Data
  Kusugak, Michael
    Hide and sneak
  ISBN 1-55037-229-7 (bound) ISBN 1-55037-228-9 (pbk.)

  1. Inuit–Juvenile fiction.* I. Krykorka, Vladyana.
  II. Title.

  PS8571.U78H5 1992 jC813'.54 C91-095479-8
  PZ7.K87Hi 1992

Distributed in Canada by: Published in the U.S.A. by Annick Press (U.S.) Ltd.
Firefly Books Ltd.   Distributed in the U.S.A. by:
3680 Victoria Park Avenue   Firefly Books (U.S.) Inc.
Willowdale, ON   P.O. Box 1338
M2H 3K1   Ellicott Station
    Buffalo, NY 14205

Printed and bound in Canada by Friesens, Altona, Manitoba.

visit us at: **www.annickpress.com**

To my wife, Sandra, with love   M.K.

For my friends in Rankin Inlet   V.K.

THE IJIRAQ AND THE INUKSUGAQ

There was once an Ijiraq who, like all other Ijiraqs, loved to play hide-and-seek. But most of all he liked to help little kids hide, and when he hid little kids, they were never ever found again. That, of course, is what Ijiraqs do: they help you hide, and when they help you hide, no one ever finds you again.

But our Ijiraq was a little different from other Ijiraqs: he was always getting lost. Whenever he went out to hide kids, he could not find his way home. And his friends teased him:

> Funny little Ijiraq
> Getting lost among the rocks
> Naa-na-na-na-naa...

He was so embarrassed. One day he decided to build an inuksugaq (which is sometimes called an inukshuk) near his home. On a hill, he piled big heavy rocks on top of each other until they looked like a man, standing. Inuksugaqs were built in a long line to corral caribou to a place where they could be hunted, but our Ijiraq used his to help him find his way home. And he never got lost again.

And to this very day that is what inuksugaqs are used for: to help you find your way home. But that is another story...

One fine summer day Allashua said, "I am going out to play hide-and-seek, Mom."

Her mother said, "Don't go too far away. An Ijiraq might hide you, and if an Ijiraq hides you, no one will ever find you again."

ᐅᑭᕈᑕ ᑕᐅ�<ᖅᑲᑦ

"Yes, Mom," Allashua said, and went out of her tent into the sunshine. Tiny flowers covered the ground, and the water on the lake behind her tent was so still she could see the sky in it. A loon made a long "V" in the water as it swam on the lake. On the sea in front of her tent, the floats on a net were lined up neatly in the still water. When all the floats are floating on the water there are no fish in the nets. They were all floating.

On a hill an inuksugaq stood quietly looking out over the land and sea. It had to stand quietly because it was made of rocks, piled one on top of the other to look like a man. Allashua looked at it and wondered why anyone would pile big, heavy rocks on top of each other to look like a man. She said to herself, "I'll have to remember to ask my father what it is for." But, of course, she forgot.

S he ran off to play hide-and-seek with her friends.

Allashua loved to play hide-and-seek, but she was not very good at it. As she skipped along, looking for a place to hide, a bright yellow butterfly fluttered by and Allashua ran after it, yelling, "Qitusuk, qitusuk, qitusuk..." That, of course, is the way you make a butterfly so tired it will fall down so you can catch it. But soon Allashua got so tired she had to stop and sit down. And she forgot to hide. Allashua was not very good at hide-and-seek.

ᐅᓚᖅᐸᒃᐴᓗ

When Allashua was looking for a place to hide again, she came to a pond beside a rocky hill. Tiny, prickly fish darted across the pond floor and disappeared under the rocks. She stopped to take a closer look. There was a big black bug crawling along the pond floor. It looked like a beetle, just meandering along on its short black legs. Then there were teeny, tiny fish that she thought looked like they did not have any skins at all. She could see their skeletons and all their insides. They swam around, just the same, without a care in the world. There were little, round, red bugs that moved about from here to there with no sign of any legs or fins. But she was most fascinated by the ulikapaalik, a tiny, turtle-like creature in a fragile-looking shell. It had a pointy tail and swam along by tickling the water with the many fingers on its underside. Allashua watched these bugs for a long time. And she completely forgot to hide again.

And again she lost her turn. She was not very good at hide-and-seek.

Later, when Allashua was looking for a place to hide, she came upon a nest of tiny baby birds. The baby birds lifted their tiny beaks up to her and chirped, "Cheep, cheep, cheep, cheep..."

Allashua got on her knees, puckered up her lips and replied, "Cheep, cheep, cheep..."

And from somewhere behind her, Allashua heard some whistling and a tiny voice, singing:

Hide-and-sneak, hide-and-sneak
How I love to hide-and-sneak...

Allashua looked around, but there was no one there. There were rocks and flowers and Old-squaw ducks on a lake, but they weren't whistling or singing. She scratched her head and went back to the little birds. She puckered up her lips again to talk to them, but, behind her, there was the little voice again:

Hide-and-sneak, hide-and-sneak
How I love to hide-and-sneak
I hide and you seek
You won't find me for a week.

Allashua looked around. She didn't see anybody, but she heard the whistling and singing and laughing, like someone was having a good time. She looked and looked and, finally, behind a big rock, she found a tiny little man. He was dressed in a fur coat that looked like ptarmigan feathers in summer. His brown legs were bare and he had nothing on his feet at all. Like a ptarmigan in summer, he was very hard to see. Allashua knew she had met an Ijiraq, a hide-and-seek creature.

The little man laughed and cackled and danced as he sang his little song. As soon as he saw Allashua he skipped away to hide behind a rock, but as he did so he tripped on the rock and went tumbling along the ground. Allashua laughed and ran after him. He was a shy little man, but soon he began to play with Allashua. He loved to play hide-and-seek, and he was very good at it.

Allashua said, "I am not very good at hiding."

The Ijiraq said, "I am very good at hiding. Let me help you."

ᐅᑭᐅᖅᑕᕐᑐᖅᑐᑎᒡ

Dedicated to cat lovers everywhere.

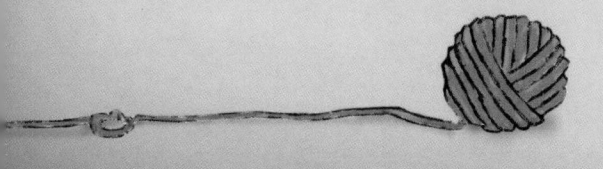

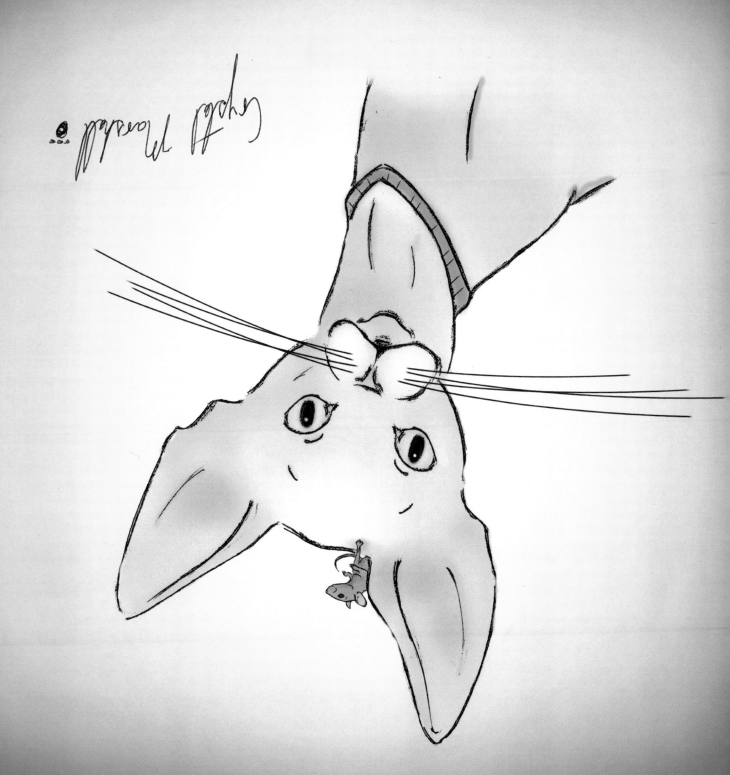

$\mathcal{O}$nce upon time there lived a cat named Percy. He was no ordinary cat… he was a Chinese Hairless Cat. Being a cat did not bother Percy, nor did being Chinese, but what made him uncomfortable was the fact that he did not have any fur, and he had to wear sweaters so he wouldn't catch cold.

Everyday he would sit on the windowsill of his apartment and look out at all the other cats below, enjoying the sun in the nearby park. He wished he could frolic and play with the others, but he was too shy and embarrassed to do so. He thought that the other cats would make fun of him.

One of the cats that played in the park was Creampuff, a beautiful Persian, whose fur was like a fluffy white cloud. She happened to live in the same apartment building as Percy. Sometimes they would see each other while their owners talked. Percy was so embarrassed of his furlessness, especially when he was next to Creampuff, that he would hide behind Grandma Meow's legs and howl until she let him back inside.

Percy's life went on like this for many months until one morning.......
While entering the kitchen for breakfast, Percy was met nose-to-nose with Cream-puff! She was actually in his home! What was she doing here!? Percy made a hasty retreat by slipping and sliding over the kitchen tile, making quite the exit scene. Flabbergasted, Creampuff just stood there. It had all happened so fast, she didn't know if Percy had actually been there or if she had just imagined the whole thing.

It seemed as though Creampuff's owner had gone away for a while and, much to Percy's dismay, Creampuff was going to stay in the apartment until his return. Percy did not like this one bit! Sure, when he had the apartment to himself he was lonely, but at least he didn't have anyone looking at him, especially the fluffiest furball there ever was. He spent most of his days now hiding under his bed.

A few days after the kitchen encounter, Percy saw Creampuff heading his way. He cowered in the shadows, hoping that she would not see him, but it was too late. As Creampuff approached, she nervously pawed the floor before speaking to Percy.

"Hi there, Percy," she greeted, smiling shyly.

"Hi, Creampuff," Percy sneered, peering out from under the shadows. He tried hard not to stare at her luscious white fur coat. "I was wondering if you could tell me the secret of your magical fur?" Creampuff asked.

Percy was, to say the least, surprised. "You mean my sweater?" He gasped and sat up, bonking his head on the underside of the bed. Creampuff did not understand.
"Sweaters....what are sweaters?
Don't you have magical fur?"
She asked.

Percy emerged from under the bed and explained to Creampuff what a sweater was, and why he had to wear one.

He took off the sweater he was wearing to show that he was, indeed, quite hairless. Creampuff pinkened from embarrassment. But as soon as a draft passed through the room, Percy had to put the sweater back on because he was chilly.

6

Creampuff didn't mind that his fur wasn't magical, she still thought it was a nifty idea to wear a sweater and that he looked rather spiffy in his.

Percy wasn't as embarrassed as he had been and decided to share his sweaters with Creampuff. He opened a dresser drawer, revealing a mountain of fabric. Percy invited Creampuff to try on as many sweater–creations as she wanted.

She tried on hoodie sweaters, turtleneck sweaters, holiday sweaters with dangling ornaments, oversized sweaters with pooling arms, and teeny tiny sweaters that made her fur pop out and eyes bulge. There were sweaters of every color and design! Creampuff tried them all on, even the monogrammed one that Grandma Meow made that was secretly Percy's favorite. Even though Creampuff sampled them all, none of them felt quite right. However, she wanted to look just like Percy, so she settled on the red one with yellow triangles.

7

"Let's go to the park!" Creampuff suggested, eager to show off her new look to the other park cats. Percy was nervous to go outside and wondered what the other cats would think of him, but being with beautiful Creampuff gave him courage. He agreed, and they hopped out the window together.

The two cats made their way to the park, where the others were playing. The park cats stopped as Percy and Creampuff walked by. They thought the two looked silly wearing clothes. None of the park cats had heard about a Chinese Hairless Cat. The park cats began to laugh at Percy and Creampuff. They tried to ignore them and continue having fun, but the park cats started to tease.

"Hey Miss Creamy-Puff," they howled.

"Why is such a cool cat like you hanging out with Mr. Nooooo-Fur?"

Percy and Creampuff stopped their playing while other cats circled around them.

"You're looking different today Creampuff....is it the....SWEATER?!

Ha-ha-haha-ha," they sang.

"Creampuff is the sweater-cat and Percy is the bald cat."

Creampuff and Percy weren't having fun anymore. They were about to cry.

As nervous as Percy was about being outside and being with the other cats, he knew teasing wasn't right, and decided to stand up for himself and his friend.

"Hey, you hair balls, Creampuff is my friend, and we are going to play in this park! Stop making fun of us! I think that wearing sweaters is fun and I think that Creampuff looks very beautiful in her's!"

The park cats were surprised to hear how Percy was talking to them. They stuttered and stammered before running away.

"Thanks for standing up for me, Percy," Creampuff sniffled, while wiping her eyes. "All I wanted was to look like you... but all we got was trouble."

Percy patted her back in a "there-there" sort of way. "Why did you want to look like me? I'm so different from all the other cats."

"Well," Creampuff explained, "It's because you never look the same as the day before and if you ever get too warm, you can always take off your sweater. I'm stuck with this one fur."

"Really?" Percy gasped. "I had no idea. I sometimes get jealous of you because you never get cold and your fur is so beautiful."

The two cats paused for a moment, realizing what the other had said.
"Let's just be happy being ourselves." Percy suggested.
Creampuff nodded, and they gave each other a big kitty-hug.

"I guess it's alright to be yourself,"
she said, while walking back to
their apartment.
"Of course it's okay.
It's great to be who we are,
and we shouldn't try to be
anyone else."
"Because cats come in all
shapes, sizes, and colors,"
Creampuff added.
"That they do,"
Percy nodded.
"That they do."

They both went to bed that night, all snuggled in tight on the windowsill,
with Percy in his sweater and Creampuff with her fur coat,
happy being exactly who they were.

The End

Made in the USA
Charleston, SC
28 September 2012

Allashua thought, "This guy is an Ijiraq, and my mother said if an Ijiraq hides you, no one will ever find you again. But he is such a happy, fun-loving little man. Elves don't hide you forever; dwarves don't hide you forever; leprechauns don't hide you forever. I think my mother is wrong."

She said, "Okay."

Allashua and the Ijiraq skipped up the hill with the inuksugaq on it. As they skipped down the other side, the Ijiraq tripped on a rock again and went tumbling down. Allashua laughed and laughed. He was so funny. They skipped and sang across a rocky field. They skipped around a lake. They skipped and danced through a big field of cotton grass. Finally, they came to a small creek with fish fins sticking up out of the water. As they stepped into the water to skip across, the fish jumped and water splashed everywhere. They skipped across and hid in a cave that Allashua had never seen before. Allashua looked all around. She did not have the foggiest idea where they were. She asked, "Where are we? I have never seen this place before."

The Ijiraq replied, "We are in my special hiding place. Here no one will ever find us."

They hid. They hid for a long time. The Ijiraq beamed with pride at being such a good hider. Lunchtime came and went, and still no one found them. The Ijiraq laughed and cackled and sang his little song. He was having a wonderful time. But Allashua was getting hungry. She decided that no one would ever find them again and that it suited the Ijiraq just fine. She said, "I want to go home now."

The Ijiraq replied, "But they haven't found us yet."

"I am hungry and I want to go home now!" Allashua insisted.

"Well, you can't!" the Ijiraq said, getting annoyed at Allashua.

Allashua wanted to go home. She was getting awfully hungry, and now she missed her mother, too. But the Ijiraq was not going to let her go home.

Then she had a terrific idea. She looked straight at the Ijiraq and said to him, "You look funny."

The Ijiraq looked at her and said, "Don't look at me!"

But Allashua kept right on staring at him. "Your nose is crooked," she said, teasing the Ijiraq.

The Ijiraq's face turned red, he was so shy. But Allashua kept staring straight at him. She could not look away now; if she did, she knew he would disappear. "Don't look at me!" he said again.

Y ou're a clumsy little oaf, always tripping over things," she said.

"Don't stare at me!" he said. His face was red hot.

"Only if you take me home," she said.

"No!" he said again.

"Red face, red face, reddest in the human race. Naa, na, na, na, na..." Allashua teased.

Well, the Ijiraq was so shy he could not stand it any longer. He said, "Okay, I'll take you home, but don't stare at me anymore."

They left the cave. They skipped along again until they came to the tiny creek. There were the fish again, their fins sticking up out of the shallow water. Even before her feet touched the water, Allashua knew something was going to happen. —But it was too late: she did not dare take her eyes away from the Ijiraq. They jumped into the water. The fish jumped up, splashing water everywhere. The water splashed on Allashua's dress, it splashed on Allashua's hair and it splashed into Allashua's eyes. Allashua blinked. When she opened her eyes, the Ijiraq was gone. Poof. Gone. Just like that.

Allashua looked around, but the Ijiraq was nowhere to be found. She looked everywhere. Still there was no Ijiraq. Allashua was alone. And she didn't know where she was. She was lost.

Allashua began to cry, "Waah, I want my Mommy... Waa-ah, I want to go home..."

She cried for a long time, but no one came. She cried until her eyes turned as red as the Ijiraq's face. She cried until she had no cry left in her body. Then, finally, she stopped crying.

A llashua didn't know what to do. She looked all around. Way, way far away, so far away she could hardly see it, there was a black dot on a hill. It was the only thing she saw on the horizon. Allashua wondered what it was. She said to herself, "I am going to go there."

She started to walk. She walked across a field of cotton grass. The black dot on the hill looked a little bigger. She skipped around a lake. Now the black dot on the hill seemed to be standing. She skipped and danced across a large rocky field. Now the dot looked like a man standing on the hill. She went up the hill and walked over to it. It was an inuksugaq, standing quietly, looking out over the land and sea. She said, "I have seen this inuksugaq before." She looked around to where the inuksugaq was looking. There was a river, there was the sea and the land and, way down on the shore, there was a tent. She looked and looked at the tent. It was her tent. She was so happy. She said, "Thank you," to the inuksugaq and skipped and ran all the way home.

ᐅᐁ ᑳᑦᒐᐅᑌᖅᑯ ᒪᕐᖓ

H er mother and father and brothers and sisters were so happy to see her. They hugged her and kissed her and asked, "Where have you been, Allashua? We have been worried about you."

"On the other side of the hill, playing hide-and-seek," she replied.

She told them about playing hide-and-seek, she told them about the Ijiraq and she told them about being lost. Then she asked her father, "Father, what is an inuksugaq for?"

"To help you find your way home," he replied.

She said, "You know what, Father? It works."

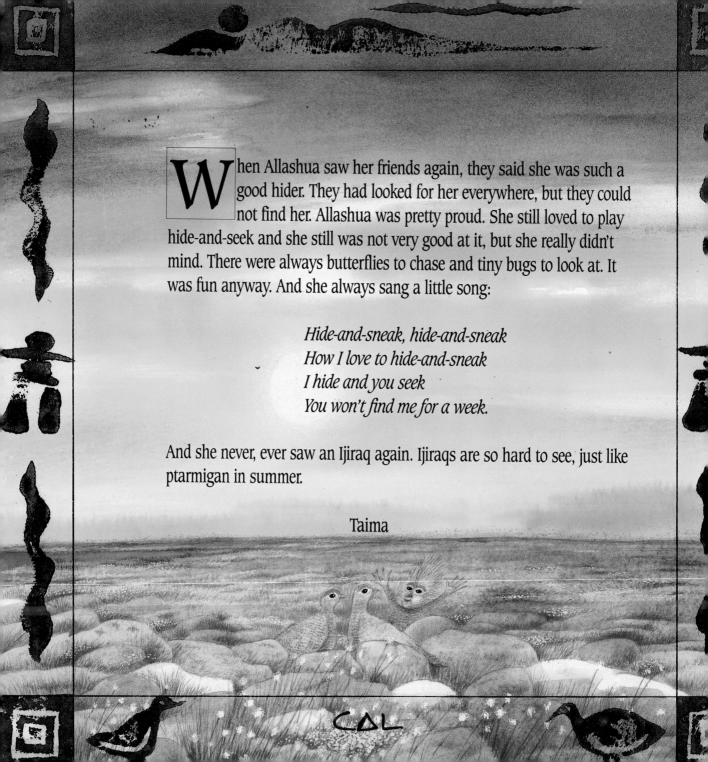

When Allashua saw her friends again, they said she was such a good hider. They had looked for her everywhere, but they could not find her. Allashua was pretty proud. She still loved to play hide-and-seek and she still was not very good at it, but she really didn't mind. There were always butterflies to chase and tiny bugs to look at. It was fun anyway. And she always sang a little song:

Hide-and-sneak, hide-and-sneak
How I love to hide-and-sneak
I hide and you seek
You won't find me for a week.

And she never, ever saw an Ijiraq again. Ijiraqs are so hard to see, just like ptarmigan in summer.

Taima